RALPH

FLYING HOUND

RALPH

FLYING HOUND

written by

DAVE PADDON

illustrated by

ALEX KOLANO

To all the bush pilots who flew (or still fly) in Labrador

~ D. P.

To my mom and dad for believing in and nurturing my artistic vision, and to November who couldn't have been more supportive and helpful even if she tried

~ a. k.

"This is a true story."

~ Dave Paddon

"Yes, it is."

~ Greg Baikie

Now my buddy Greg is an old chopper pilot,
And he flies from Goose Bay, Labrador.
Nobody knows just how long he's been at it,
But I think that he once knew Igor.

Sikorsky, I mean, who invented the things
And who gave all of mankind a lift.
You'll know what I mean if you're arse over kettle,
Crumpled up at the base of a cliff.

Or you're out at the fish in that old butter dish
With that motor that never worked right –
Next thing you know, Search and Rescue's right o-
ver your head on a dark stormy night.

But there's others involved in this tale of flight,

A tale so amazing but true.

They got four legs each, they're a bunch of hard tickets,

And between them got five tails, too.

Five tough little crackies from the Labrador coast,
They're clever and right full of gall.
Spot 1 and Lucky, Spot 2, Nance and Ralph,
But Ralph is the smartest of all.

Ralph is their leader and he's brown just like Nance,
While Lucky's as black as a pot.
Spot 1 is black with brown spots here and there;
Spot 2 hasn't got either spot.

Williams Harbour, Labrador is their place of abode,
Where they live the dog's life to be sure.
They're never tied on, got the run of the town,
Every house, every stage head and store.

Now Ralph, I suppose, is partly retriever
And he loves going after the ducks.
He'll go after just about anything that went,
Balls, sticks or pond-hockey pucks.

But with all of the things that Ralph had retrieved,
There was one thing he hadn't got yet.
And being the hard-headed fellow he was,
That's the one thing he just had to get.

'Twas a big orange duck and it made quite the racket
Every time that it came and pitched down.
And it used to spit humans, then eat them again,
Whenever it showed up in town.

"I'm having that" is what Ralphie would say,
Whenever the thing would show up.
The other dogs didn't think much of his chances,
But Ralphie was one stubborn pup.

So one day in the spring, Greg was doing his thing
And flying a trip to the coast.
He was never a man to mind much where he went,
But one place he disliked more than most.

Williams Harbour, by name, was a bit of a pain
Because of that pack of wild dogs.
Landings and take-offs were always a hazard,
Right up there with snowstorms and fogs.

Sure enough, once again, as he came in to land,
They showed up to ruin his day.
And so you're aware of what pilots fear
There's one thing I suppose I should say.

See a chopper's tail rotor's a delicate thing,
And if damaged control could be lost.
So a thirty-pound dog jumping into the thing
Is a thing to avoid at all cost.

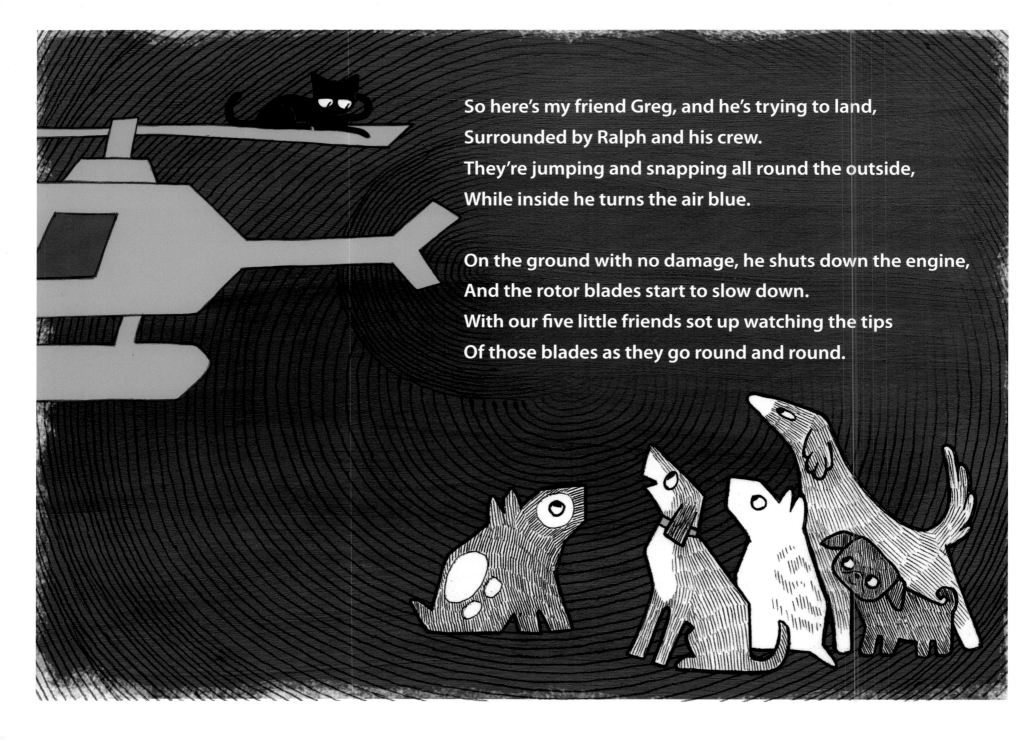

So here's my friend Greg, and he's trying to land,
Surrounded by Ralph and his crew.
They're jumping and snapping all round the outside,
While inside he turns the air blue.

On the ground with no damage, he shuts down the engine,
And the rotor blades start to slow down.
With our five little friends sot up watching the tips
Of those blades as they go round and round.

When the blades stop at last and the fun is all past,
The crackies jump up and make off.
Greg blows his stack 'cause he knows they'll be back
When it's time to start up and take off.

Sure enough, right on cue, here comes Ralph and his crew
As Greg starts his engine to leave.
Five heads rotate at an increasing rate
As the rotor blades come up to speed.

Now he's set to depart and our poor pilot's heart
Is up in the back of his throat.
With dogs jumping and leaping, the words that he's speaking
Are words that I really can't quote.

Airborne at last, with the danger all past,
He starts to move forward to leave.
And here, I'll allow, that what you'll hear now
Is something you might not believe!

See, the place where he parked was a nice level part
About eighty feet back from the shore,
And where land meets sea is a nice drop, you see –
Oh, I suppose, ten feet or more.

As he flew towards the drop, the excitable lot
Of canines had their eyes on his chopper.
And he suddenly sensed a chance for vengeance
In a way not *entirely* proper.

Well, the plan worked just right and a wonderful sight
Did our long-suffering pilot behold.
Four dogs took the fall, for the sins of them all,
Into the salt water so cold.

Greg let out a cheer as he flew through the air,
And he watched the four dogs swim ashore.
He had his revenge on the four-legged friends,
And he figured he'd evened the score.

But wait now, you say, with four dogs in the bay
What happened to our other puppy?
Both Spots went in, Nance was soaked to the skin,
And so was poor unlucky Lucky.

Ah, but Ralph was too swift to go over that cliff –
Yes, Ralph was both smarter and bolder.
Greg was into his climb when, just at that time,
He felt a light tap on his shoulder.

A passenger was pointing out to the right float –
This chopper had pontoons, you see.
They're flat on the top with a re-enforced spot
That you step on to get in or leave.

Well, sir, such a sight did our pilot behold
When he looked out the window that day.
'Twas Ralphie stretched out on the top of the float:
A bird dog, I guess you could say.

The chopper was picking up speed at the time,
And Ralph was hung on pretty tight.
With his tongue flapping 'round at the back of his head
Like the tail at the back of a kite.

With his ears flapping, too, as he took in the view
Through his eyes narrowed right down to slits.
And his bushy old tail, all astray in the gale,
Looking like a birch broom in the fits.

Greg figured much faster would lead to disaster
For his canine hitchhiker, for sure.
And, of course, that would mean one less dog on the team,
And, for Greg, less was better than more.

But he's a softhearted guy as he roars 'round the sky,
And really would not hurt a flea.
So, there just was no way, he'd go faster that day
And dump poor old Ralph in the sea.

He landed again and put off his new friend,
Who was glad to get back on the ground.
The others were waiting and anticipating
The story of *Ralph: Flying Hound*.

And so now, my friends, I suppose I should end
This tale of courage and pluck.
Canine legend will say that Ralph won the day
When he brought back that big orange duck.

Thanks to Greg Baikie, who told me the tale.

Thanks to my wife Kim, who has grown used to me mumbling and staring off into space as I try to make two lines rhyme.

Thanks to Marnie, alex and Veselina for creating this beautiful book!

~ Dave Paddon

Thanks to Dave Paddon, Veselina Tomova and Marnie Parsons for giving me this opportunity.

~ alex kolano

Born and raised in Northwest River, Labrador, **Dave Paddon** worked as a commercial pilot for many years. In 2008, he began writing and performing recitations, wonderfully comical poems in the tall-tale tradition, inspired by everyday life in Newfoundland and Labrador and by the recitations he heard as a child. Paddon is much sought after to perform at storytelling events and festivals across the province. He has published five recitations as individual, letterpress-printed chapbooks. *Ralph, Flying Hound* is his first full-length publication and his first children's book.

alex kolano grew up on a farm near Iona Station, Ontario. Born with a pen in her hand, she has been drawing since infancy. She has honed her skills through seven years of art school (three years of illustration at OCADU and four years of animation at Sheridan). Her passions include the wilderness, wildlife, books and Canadian art. *Ralph, Flying Hound* is her first picture book.

Designed by Veselina Tomova of Vis-à-Vis Graphics,
St. John's, Newfoundland and Labrador
Printed in Canada

We acknowledge the Canada Council for the Arts
for its financial support of our trade publishing program.

978-1-927917-08-4

Running the Goat
Books & Broadsides
50 Cove Road
Tors Cove, NL A0A 4A0

www.runningthegoat.com